Right Time Wrong Place

Upstate Mystery

fj donohue

Published by fj donohue, 2021.

Also by fj donohue

Endwell Investigations
Full Circle
Vindication

Upstate Mystery
Hit and Run
Two Murders by the River
A Serial Killer Returns
Right Time Wrong Place
The Caribbean Laundry

Upstate Mystery #2
Closure

Upstate Mystery #7
The Snowbird Bank Robber

Watch for more at https://upstatemystery.com.

Table of Contents

Right Place Wrong Time
An Upstate Mystery

F J Donohue

Prologue

BRIAN REYNOLDS AND Janet Codington walked down the hallway to their rooms at Edgewood Gardens Senior Living Center. They lived in the same wing, four doors down from each other. Before Janet went into her room, they agreed to meet with friends for dinner at 6. Brian went on to his room to catch up on some emails. He was in his room less than twenty minutes when there was a commotion near Janet's room. She was dead.

Chapter 1

SEAN MCCARTHY HAD BEEN at Binghamton High School longer than any of the other coaches, so he was the go-to-guy for discussions and decisions on athletic policy in the department. He had a good reputation for being sensible, and the other coaches valued his opinions.

They were having a pre-season meeting, talking about the upcoming school year and how their teams looked for the new season. After the usual chatter, the elephant in the room emerged as usually happens before the start of each season.

Marcel Argentaru, the hockey coach bought it up. "Guys, we really have to do something this year to manage team administration and all the sports equipment properly. At some point in every season I get overwhelmed with the equipment and frankly don't know where it all is! Some of it the kids are allowed to keep, some gets used again, some disappears, some is broken. I could go on forever. Depending on your sport the problem is serious or just an annoyance. On top of that, the paperwork keeps growing!"

"For sure," said Junior Roberts, the basketball coach, "my problem isn't as big, but it's still a pain in the keister."

"Agreed," said Sean. "I've thought about it yet again and have a suggestion. I would like to see us expand the role of the team managers. Typically, it's a kid who is not an athlete but wants to be part of the team. Their role is not well defined and mostly they make sure accurate scoring data is recorded and lug equipment around. Let's expand their role and give them a real job. I think that's where Marcel is headed."

"A real job, such as?" asked Marcel.

"Let's put in place a process for monitoring everything of importance to each team."

"Okay, how do we do that?", asked Sue Higgins, the girls swim team coach.

Sean replied, "Each team will have a spreadsheet with all the equipment, team statistics, player metrics, game schedules, practices and player academic information. That will be the baseline for the team. The team manager will manage and update the spreadsheet as required. It will be a bit different for each team depending on the complexity of their sport in terms of equipment and size of the team. But the team manager will be the focal point for the overall administration of the team."

Junior asked, "Sean how do we develop a spreadsheet to handle all of that?, We'll need to find some nine-year-old kids who can take some time away for their video games!"

"Well there's a guy I know, Brian Reynolds. He is the father of Tommy Reynolds, the great player we had here some years back. He's a retired CPA, used to be a partner in an accounting firm in town. He's a good computer head. He bought his firm quickly into the digital accounting world when most of the old boys were happy with paper, pens and green eye shades. I see Tommy on and off during the year when he's in town. I can call Tommy and see if he thinks it's a good idea to approach his dad about this."

"How do we bring this online?" asked Susan. We can't just give the managers a spreadsheet and turn them loose."

"Agreed," said Sean, "we'll have Brian spend time with the managers developing the spreadsheets and also populating them. The managers have to be part of the solution. Also, Brian will meet with them periodically to sort out any problems."

"So, if you want, I'll call Tommy and see what he thinks."

"Do it!" replied the chorus!

Chapter 2

TOMMY WAS IN COURT when Sean first called; he returned the call later in the day.

"Coach, this is an unexpected pleasure, is everything okay?"

"All is well, Tommy, just need to ask a question."

"Shoot".

"We are trying to bring some order to the management of our various teams at the high school. We do a good job keeping track of scores and player metrics, but the equipment side and academic performance has always been a mess. By the end of the season, the equipment is all over the place and we don't know what we have anymore. We never really hear about a player's grades until after the problem has surfaced. I want to make the role of the team manager for all our high school sports more important and have them manage the schedules, player metrics, academic performance and team equipment. My vision is some kind of spreadsheet where each team manager can keep control of all the moving parts. Your dad is a CPA and I think he would be really helpful working with our team managers putting this in place. He was always good with computers and I'm sure that's still the case. His CPA background will blend in well with this process. What do you think about me approaching him?"

"I think he would love to get involved. I'm not sure of his schedule these days other than an antique car project."

"Antique car?" said Sean. "You're kidding!"

"Not really. You know he's in Assisted Living. Well, the husband of a friend of his at Edgewood Gardens Senior Living Center died about four years ago and his wife is tired of paying storage fees on a car he had in storage for many years. She wants to sell it and dad is helping her."

"Thank you, Brian!" said Sean.

"Here's where it gets interesting," said Tommy. "The car is a 1960 Edsel Ranger convertible. They only made seventy-six of them that year and only twenty-five are known to be around today. So, the car is rare and worth some serious money!"

"How much do you think?"

"Dad says at least $125,000 and maybe a lot more depending on the usual stuff like mileage, rust and overall condition. His friend Janet says it's been in storage forever, so maybe it's a cream puff. Dad is just looking into it but thinks they should recondition it and take it to some local and regional shows to build up interest and then sell it. They don't want to put it into the large car auctions as they charge too much in commissions."

Tommy continued, "I think the reconditioning will take a lot more time than they think so there should be a lot of down time waiting for things to get finished. My guess is he'll have plenty of time for you guys."

"Okay I'll call him and tell him his son said to do it!"

"Maybe just call him and ask?"

"Good idea, Tommy."

Sean and Tommy finished the call talking about his dad and how he was doing. Tommy was happy with the family situation. His dad was happily settled in at Edgewood Gardens and had a good circle of friends. His health was good and he was active. He spent time with Tommy, Ruth and the girls in Harrisburg where Tommy worked as the lead prosecutor in the Attorney General's office. Tommy was also up in Binghamton every month or so.

Sean called Brian Reynolds at Edgewood Gardens the next day.

"Mr. Reynolds, this is Sean McCarthy from Binghamton High School. It has been some time, but I hope you remember me?"

"Sure I do, Coach," said Brian, "Tommy is always talking about you. I think he actually adopted you!"

"He's a great kid, I was so lucky to have him on our team. They don't make many kids like Tommy these days!"

"Always a joy," said Brian, "never a moment of trouble for us growing up. So, what can I do for you, Coach?"

Sean explained to Brian what he wanted to do with the team managers. Give them a bigger administrative role, and finally get the team equipment under control. Brian was intrigued by the idea and Sean could almost feel him working out a solution as they spoke. Sean explained that he would need him to work with the managers designing a system, populating it, launching it and some level of ongoing care and maintenance.

"Coach, I have a car project going but am sure I can fit this in. I don't think the car will be finished until the Spring, so plenty of time."

"Thanks, Brian, let me get the team managers together. We can meet and take the next steps. I'll be back to you shortly."

Chapter 3

SEAN HAD THE SCHOOL administration put out a notice to the students advising that anyone interested in being a team manager for a particular sport, contact their respective coach. Each coach would make their team manager selection. When Sean got to his office the next day, Carlita Suarez was waiting at his office door.

"Coach, I want to apply to be the team manager for football"

"Okay, but can I tell you a bit about the job and responsibilities and also can you tell me a bit about yourself. Let's see if we have a fit."

"You first," said Carlita.

"No way," said the coach, "I'm buying, you're selling. Tell me about the package!"

"Coach, I know you don't want a girl as manager, but I am going to change your mind."

"Whoa, Carlita! I don't care if you're Mother Theresa or Atilla the Hun. I care about having someone who will be with me all season and work to implement an enhanced team management system. I'm not looking for someone to carry the footballs and shine the helmets. I want a hands-on manager who will be respected by the team and make a solid contribution to our success. There's nothing sexist about this job, you can take that off the table."

"I'm sorry, Coach. I fight this battle with my brothers all the time. I thought if I can work for the football team, I can get them to back down."

"Okay, tell me about yourself and what you want to do."

Carlita said, "I love computers and want to major in computer science when I graduate. After that, I want to start my own company. Not sure if it will be a hardware or a software product line but definitely computers."

Sean asked, "Do you code?"

"Is the Pope catholic?" answered Carlita.

"Then, I assume you know spreadsheets?"

"Sure do, use them all the time."

"Okay", said the coach. "I'll take you on. You'll have to have a thick skin as I suspect there might be some pushback from the administration and ballplayers about having a female football manager. I'll handle the administration; you got the rest."

"Can do, Coach," Carlita said, "with 2 older brothers I have fought this battle many times."

"One very important thing, Carlita," said Sean, "you must tell me if anyone ever crosses the line with you. Understood?"

"Thanks Coach, nice to know someone has my back. By the way, everyone calls me Carly."

The following Monday there was a meeting in a corner of the gym for all the team managers and interested coaches. Sean introduced Brian Reynolds explaining that he would be working with the managers to develop a comprehensive system to manage the teams and the player activities. The kids were excited to be part of something new. Marcel Argentaru, the hockey coach, was at the meeting and volunteered to be the interface for the other coaches. He had been offering keyboard and coding classes that the students could take during study periods. Just go to the computer lab and sign in for the courses. It was very popular. Marcel had a good relationship with the students. He respected them and they reciprocated.

Brian started out by outlining the steps he thought they needed to take to put the system in place. "Let's define what data we need to track. Scoring metrics, equipment, grades, etc. Once we have that in place, we can develop a system. I think it should be spreadsheet based to give us flexibility in using it and more importantly, modifying and updating it as we go forward. So, for the next meeting, list all the data points you think we need to track. We can skinny it down to a workable database and go forward."

"When do we meet again?" Carly asked.

"After school, day after tomorrow," said Brian. "I live at Edgewood Gardens which is two blocks from here. We can meet there. I can book meeting space and they have a pretty good internet setup. Also, free soda and snacks! We probably can also meet at the school library if you want. But not with snacks."

"Free soda and snacks! I vote for Edgewood Gardens", said Bobby Miller the hockey manager.

"Done", replied Brian.

The initial meeting at Edgewood Gardens was quite an event for the place. A room full of high school kids with loads of energy and enthusiasm. The residents were happy to see them and curious as to what was going on. The kids eagerly engaged with the residents and it was like a party atmosphere. Brian told Linda, the day manager, to make sure that there were plenty of soda and snacks for their meeting. He would cover the cost. The first meeting was a bit like herding cats. Lots of good ideas and lots of, what to say—well less than good ideas! Brian let the kids decide on what they would track and, in the end, they came to a good place. He didn't want to dictate to them what data was in or out of the spreadsheet. When they finalized their data inputs, Brian asked them to list the resources they would need to access to keep the data current. The main issue was student performance. The managers wanted to be able to look ahead and anticipate an academic problem. Not wait for the report cards.

Marcel, who was part of the meeting, spoke up. "Let me run with this. I'll get with Coach Sean and we'll meet with the Vice Principal for academics. What you are looking for is some input from the guidance counselors or teachers that a student is on the wrong side of the curve. Do I have this right?"

"That's it," said Carly, "we want to be proactive and provide help and resources."

"Okay, let me work on it."

They agreed to meet in two days and try to populate one of the team spreadsheets. Marcel offered the hockey team as it has lots of moving parts. Although less complex than the football team, the hockey team also had a fair number of players and equipment. Size wise, it was a good place to start. He also thought that he and Sean should be able to get the academic side of this sorted out by then and the other elements of the spreadsheet were pretty well defined. They agreed to continue to meet at Edgewood Gardens as the place had passed the soda and snack test! After the meeting ended, the kids were in no hurry to leave. They stayed around talking among themselves and also with the residents. *Maybe they found some new friends here?* thought Brian.

Chapter 4

BRIAN AND JANET HAD dinner that evening with Bill and Maggie Wilson, also residents of Edgewood Gardens. All the talk around the place was about the kids meeting there and their energy. Brad explained what they were trying to put into place; a comprehensive system to track equipment and events over a period of time.

"You know," said Maggie, we could use something like that here."

"What do you mean?"

"Well Brian, we need to track events. You know how over time people find that some of their personal stuff goes missing, especially with residents requiring comprehensive care. It never happens at once, it's always a series of occurrences over time. The seriousness of the problem is never evident and many times chalked up to the age or perceived infirmity of the resident. What if we had a tracking system that put it all in one place with dates and maybe something of a value element to the missing items?"

"Sure, that would be compelling. Hard to argue with evidence like that."

"Can you do this?' asked Maggie.

"I think so, get me the data and I'll show you how to populate a spreadsheet. Can you and Bill be the gatherers of the data? Go back as far as you feel the data is accurate and try to get as much detail as possible. Be careful with valuations as these missing items only get more valuable over time! Let's meet when you have some information and we can assess it."

"This is great," Bill said, "we're on the case!"

Sean turned to Janet. "We need to go over to Rogers Storage and look at your car. I'm not sure what needs to be done to it in terms of refurbishing it for sale. It may be too long in storage and best sold as-is instead of putting a lot of money in it that you may never recover. My sense is that we will have to have some work done on the engine, transmission and rear end as it hasn't been run in years. Also, I can imagine belts, wheel bearings, motor mounts and other rubber-based things will be dried out and need to be replaced. I've a guy in Kirkwood who looks after my Nissan Murano. His name is John Forman. We can talk to him and see what he thinks."

"Will he do the work?"

"He will but he always gets loaded up. He has a hard time saying no to his customers, so we need to be patient. I like his work and his prices are fair."

"Okay, let's do this tomorrow," said Janet.

Rogers storage was a real surprise. It was a climate-controlled environment and the car was in a large plywood enclosure. Sort of like a drive-in box! They needed one of the warehouse guys to open up the box for them. Once it was opened, Brian was amazed. The car was covered in a canvas tarp and was on jacks with the tires removed and off to the side. The inside was covered with bed sheets to protect the seats and dashboard. There was paperwork advising that the gasoline, transmission fluid, oil and engine coolant had been removed and a light oil had replaced the normal oil in the crankcase and transmission.

Brian said, "I've never seen such a complete storage job. What was George thinking?"

"Good question," said Janet, "You know he did quite well during his working career, so we did have money for toys. He ran the car for a little over a year and then said he was going to put it in storage with Rogers for a few years and then sell it off. He told me it was a limited edition and would be worth some money. That's about all I know. It just stayed there and George paid the storage fees. I can ask my son Rob; he may know more"

"Sure, you can but it doesn't really matter at this point. You've got a great car to work with. Thank you, George! I'll call Johnny and have him come take a look at it. I think this is a special car, well taken care of these past forty plus years. It's in great shape to refurbish and sell. You'll do well with this, Janet."

Johnny Forman came over later in the week and towed the car to his shop in Kirkwood. A couple of weeks later he called Brian with an assessment of the car.

"Never seen anything like this Brian. I think I'm in a time warp in a Rod Serling story."

"What are your thoughts on bringing it back?"

"Well Brian, it's worth doing and will really enhance the value. I think the paint can be buffed out. Needs a new convertible top and that's a custom-made item. There are shops that do that. I think we need to look inside the engine. I want to replace the head gaskets and overhead valve cover gaskets, so we are pretty much there in terms of opening up the engine. All the hoses and connectors, anything rubber needs to be replaced but it's all manageable. I recommend we get all the parts first and then do the work. It'll be cheaper that way."

"How much do you think it will cost?"

"I don't know and won't until I cost it all out."

"Let's do this. We'll pay you for your time to price out the job. That way if Janet does not want to go forward, you're not out-of-pocket. If she does want to do this, and I think she will, we can give you some money upfront to buy the parts."

"Thanks Brian, sure wish all my customers were like that."

As they were driving back to Edgewood Gardens Brian said to Janet, "Best give Rob a call and let him know what you're planning. He may have other thoughts."

"I spoke with him the other day and he's fine with what I'm doing. He's not a car guy. I think George offered the car to him some years back, but he wasn't interested. I think that's why it's been at Rogers for so long. George didn't want to be bothered with the car anymore and keeping it at Rogers was an easy choice. Then he became ill and that pretty much sealed it."

"How much is the storage fee?"

"Today it's $150 a month."

"Yikes, that's a lot of money. Let's sort this car out."

Janet felt a lot better about the situation. The car had been bothering her for some time. She could afford the storage fees but writing the check every month was troubling. She felt she was throwing money away. Now she had a plan and a way out of it.

Chapter 5

OVER COFFEE AND THE New York Times the next day Brian thought, *I've got a lot of balls in the air now. I need to set some priorities and not just run around tickling problems. So where am I with the projects?*

The car was in good shape with Johnny Forman. Janet had sent him a check for $500 to scope out the job. The high school kids would be back shortly and they could start populating a spreadsheet. Sean and Marcel should have the academic information on the players sorted out for the upcoming meeting. Bill and Maggie were on the hunt for data from the residents on missing items. So, let it all cook and see what comes back. Once the data came in, his priority would be to get the Binghamton High project launched as the sports seasons were on the horizon. The other two projects could move along at a more leisurely pace. He spent most of the afternoon reading a Lee Child mystery. The main character, a guy named Reacher, was the biggest, baddest, smartest guy on the planet. None of the bad boys could take him down. Great escapism. No reality to it but so much fun to read. Go get-em Reacher!

He met up with Janet for coffee later in the afternoon. They talked about the Edsel, Bill and Maggie's investigation and, of course, their kids. They grow up but they're still your kids. They walked back to their rooms in the west wing. Janet's room came first. They chatted near her door and agreed to meet up for dinner at 6 that evening. Brian's room was four rooms down from Janet. He headed there to catch up on some emails before dinner. He wasn't in his room 20 minutes when there was a commotion in the hall. He looked out and could see it was coming from Janet's room. He ran down to her room to find Carol, the day nurse, standing next to Janet's bed.

"I'm so sorry Brian," she said, "Janet is dead! Pauline from next door stopped by and found her."

"How can that be? I was with her less than twenty minutes ago!"

"I can't say at this point. We'll need to call the coroner. I need to find Linda, our day manager, to report this."

"You go find her; I'll stay here with Janet."

Brian sat by Janet trying to process what had happened. So quick, just a matter of a few minutes. She was happy and did not complain of any pain when he left her. Heart attack? Stroke? What happened? As he sat there, he started to become aware of the surroundings. Janet was lying on the bed with her shoes on. She would never do that and, in fact, always used a comfortable recliner for resting. Rob had bought it for her birthday. She was on her back with her arms at her sides, almost like she had been posed. Nobody rests on a bed like that. He did not notice any stress on her face. But there was redness about her left wrist and some abrasions. George's watch was gone! It was always with her. He looked about but did not see it on her night table or dresser. She was wearing slacks and a blouse. The blouse was wrinkled and it was not like that when he left her earlier.

Carol the RN and Linda the day manger came back and could see that Brian was having trouble coming to terms with the scene. He explained his misgivings.

Linda said, "The coroner will be here shortly, let's see what he thinks about this. I looked in Janet's file and she had pre-arrangements with Nichols Funeral Home. I need to first call her son in Albany. I'm not sure what to tell him at this point. Let me just say that his mom died. We don't know enough to draw any conclusions. I don't want to scare him with conjecture."

When the coroner arrived, Brian was still with Janet and told the coroner about his observations and concerns. Fortunately, the coroner was a MD and not a good old boy doing some part time work. The coroner looked carefully at Janet's eyes, face, and neck. There were things that made him uncomfortable. He did not talk while conducting his examination but took a lot of notes. As he concluded his examination, he asked Brian if he would make a statement to the police about what he observed.

"Sure, I will."

The coroner waited for the funeral home people to arrive and told them to not make any preparations of the body for burial until they had determined a cause of death. He told them it was an open matter at this point.

"Are you going to do an autopsy?" Brian asked.

"I'm going to talk with Lt. Raimondi. Also going to ask him to get a statement from you. Let's not get ahead of ourselves."

The coroner told Linda to close off the room and not allow anyone into it as this was a potential crime scene.

There was a lot of talk about Janet at Edgewood Gardens that evening. She was very popular and her death was a shock. Brian did not discuss any of his concerns with the other residents. He didn't want to pour gasoline on a fire. He had called Rob shortly after they took Janet to the funeral home. Rob was having trouble accepting that his mother had died. They had been in constant contact and he had no indication of any medical problems either new or ongoing. Rob and Brian agreed to keep in touch. Rob said he would be coming down to Binghamton the next day.

That night, Brian called his son in Harrisburg. "Tommy, this is just awful. So sudden and it just doesn't look right. I don't like it one bit and am sure something bad happened. She was with me minutes before. She was fine! Something's not right here Tommy!"

"Okay, Pop, what did the coroner say?"

"Well, you know he wouldn't go into detail with me, but he listened to my concerns and told me that the police would probably want me to make a statement. He also looked very carefully at Janet's eyes, face, neck and left wrist. He didn't talk to me about it, but he did take a lot of notes. He also told the funeral home people to not prepare the body for burial until he ruled on a cause of death and spoken with Detective Raimondi."

"Pop, let the cops and coroner do their job. Everything you've told me makes good sense and the coroner is following proper procedures. Raimondi is a good cop and won't let anything slip by him."

Chapter 6

BRIAN GOT A CALL THE next day from Lt. Raimondi.

"Mr. Reynolds, would you meet with us at the station and record a statement about the death of Janet Coddington?"

"I can come by around 2pm today."

"Thank you. Ask for me at the desk in the lobby. I'll tell them to expect you."

"I'm meeting with her son Rob later this morning, should I bring him with me?"

"No, we want to hear what you have to say first and also review the coroner's report before we make any decisions. I want to be on solid ground when we meet with Mr. Coddington."

Brian met with Lt. Raimondi and Detective Elton Hendricks at the station as agreed. Lt Raimondi introduced Detective Hendricks who would be the lead investigator in the case. Elton Hendricks was an African American around thirty-five years old or so. He came to Binghamton from the New York City Police Department about four years ago so the family could be closer to his wife's parents who were struggling with health issues. Elton had been with the NYPD since graduation from Fordham University in the city. He rose quickly from street patrol to detective. He had a good reputation for closing cases. Elton was around six feet tall and like everyone in his age group was fighting an expanding midsection. Exercise and his wife's careful cooking were keeping the monster at bay!

"Mr. Reynolds," said Detective Hendricks, "I'm going to ask you to record a statement for us. As you do this, please tell us only what you observed, not what you think. I know this sounds a bit rigid, but we need to be as objective as possible and not let our emotions dictate the outcome."

"I understand. Please call me Brian."

"Okay, I'm Elton and this is Phil."

"I've heard of you, Phil, from my son Tommy. He works for the Attorney General in Harrisburg."

"Oh sure, I know Tommy, our paths cross occasionally."

Elton asked, "Is he the Reynolds who played NFL ball a few years back? "I remember a Reynolds who left the NFL for the law. He was a Binghamton kid"

"That's my boy!"

"I saw him play a few times when he was with the Eagles. Great arm!"

Phil excused himself and Elton recorded the statement from Brian. It took longer than Brian thought it would and it was draining going through all the details again. It seemed as if Elton asked the same question from different angles, wanting to make sure it was as accurate as possible.

When they finished Elton said, "We'll get this transcribed, so we have a hard copy as well as a recording. We may ask you to come back to review it. Thanks for doing this, I know it was difficult."

"I wasn't ready for the trauma of going through it all again. Let me also review the transcript, I want to make sure I got it all. Janet was a sweetheart. I still can't believe she's gone. You know Elton, she was my best friend. Doesn't that sound strange? You would think there would have to be a romantic involvement, but it was not like that. We both had great marriages and were living the next phase of our lives. I loved her but it's hard to put it into context. Maybe something like a sister, some family member? I don't know. I'm not making much sense right now. Please get to the bottom of this."

After Brian left, Phil and Elton discussed his statement and the next steps. Brian's observations were troubling. By themselves maybe not conclusive, but grounds for further investigation. However, coupled with the coroner's report that raised questions as to the cause of death, it pointed to foul play. The coroner suspected suffocation and had requested an autopsy.

"I agree with the coroner's request for an autopsy."

"Me too," replied Elton. "I'll get in touch with Rob Coddington and let him know what we are doing. He's still in town. It might be helpful if Brian is with him when I update him, I'm sure he is very concerned about this and could use some backup support."

"Good idea, but make sure that Brian understands that he's there to provide emotional support. We don't want him playing junior detective."

"Okay," said Elton, "I'll set up a meeting with them for tomorrow. I also need to tell the funeral home to send the body to Binghamton General Hospital for an autopsy."

When Brian got back to Edgewood Gardens, Rob was in Linda's office. He was distraught. He could not get into his mother's room as there was an investigation going on. Brian met with him and tried to offer some comfort, but it was hard to do. He could only tell him that he had given a statement to the police but could not go into any detail. While they were talking, a call came from Detective Hendricks asking to meet with Rob the next day. Elton also asked if Brian could join the meeting.

"He's right here," said Rob, "let me put him on."

"Brian, can you join Rob tomorrow? I need you to provide emotional support. He's going through some difficult times."

"I'll be there."

"Thank you. A bit of guidance if you would let me pass it on. Don't speculate with Rob about the investigation. Let us do our jobs."

"I understand," Brian replied.

"Would you put Rob back on the phone, please."

"Mr. Coddington," said Elton, "we are concerned about the cause of death. The coroner has requested an autopsy."

"Do you have to do this?"

"We do sir. We have to determine the cause of death and an autopsy is the only way to conclusively make a determination in a case like this. Don't believe everything you hear about them in the movies or read in novels. The doctors are respectful."

Rob and Brian met with Detective Hendricks the next day. Elton explained to them where they were in the investigation. That the coroner found the death suspicious and Brian's statement provided more uncertainty. Binghamton General hospital would be performing an autopsy today. Janet's room had been sealed off and a crime scene team had been sent to Edgewood Gardens. He would also be going back to Janet's room tomorrow as part of his investigation and also interviewing Linda and Carol from the staff.

"Mr. Coddington," said Elton, "I'm sure you've more questions than we've answers at this point, but I'll try to give as much information as I can."

"Thanks Detective. Do you think mom was murdered?"

"At this point we just don't know. But we don't like what we see. The autopsy will provide the answer as to the cause of death. We should have it very soon."

"When can I have mom back so I can bury her?"

"We'll release the body as soon as the autopsy is completed. Today is Tuesday and I think Thursday is realistic, maybe even a day earlier. The funeral home will be contacted immediately."

"Who would do this? Mom was a really nice person. She didn't have any enemies, debts or anything like that. She was a warm caring person."

Rob started to sob. Brian put his arm around him to try to provide some comfort.

Elton spoke, "Mr. Coddington, we have a long way to go with this investigation and many unanswered questions at this point. It will take some time to get to the bottom of it. If there was foul play, we won't let it go, I promise you."

Chapter 7

THE NEXT DAY AFTER stopping by his office, Elton went over to Edgewood Gardens to meet with Linda and Carol. Both women had been employed there for a number of years. They were very concerned about the death of Janet especially if it was by foul play.

"This is tragic," Linda said, "I've been here over ten years and we've never had anything like this. I feel so sorry for the residents, such confusion and worry for them."

Carol said, "It's especially hard on the Senior Living residents. Janet was so well liked by them and was a dear friend. The other residents who are under more comprehensive care are not really aware of the situation, so the impact is not as severe. However, for the senior living residents, this is traumatic especially with the police involvement."

"We'll be as discreet as we can," replied Elton, "I'm hoping we can clear the room in a few days and our presence here will mainly be with you and Linda."

Elton continued, "Tell me about your security camera setup. I didn't notice any cameras in the wings or her room. I do see cameras in the lobby, dining area, and parking lots."

"We offered to install cameras in the wings," said Linda, "but the residents did not want them there. They felt it was too intrusive. Some of the residents have their own cameras installed in their rooms. We certainly support this but it's a personal decision. Only a few have opted to do this."

"How long do you keep the video?"

Linda replied, "Our security company keeps the recordings for one year. They store them at the company."

"Carol," Elton asked, "I know you've been through this before but take me through the events in finding Janet."

"Well, Pauline found her when she stopped by her room. She called the switchboard from Janet's room and they alerted me and I came to Janet's room immediately."

"Did Pauline say Janet was dead at that point?"

"She did. Pauline is a retired RN. She worked at Lourdes Hospital for years. She told me Janet was unresponsive and she could not detect a pulse or breathing."

Elton asked, "Do you think she had to move the body in the bed to determine whether she was breathing?"

"No, she was careful. A hand on the neck and wrist but that's all. She knew what she was doing. You can check with Pauline to make sure."

"Thanks, I'll see her today when I go to Janet's room. Carol, did anything stand out to you when you went to see about Janet? The body? The room?"

"Candidly, Detective Hendricks, my main interest was Janet. Was she alive? I didn't look around the room at all. I'm pretty sure it was neat and tidy as always."

"What about Janet?"

"She didn't appear to be in any distress. In fact, almost peaceful. I know this sounds a bit odd, but she had her shoes on and her position did not seem like a normal sleeping posture."

"Thank you both for your cooperation. We'll be asking you to come to my office within the week to make a formal statement."

"Do Linda and I need to have a lawyer?'

"I don't think so. We just want to make sure we capture all the information. As we go forward it's important to have factual data to refer back to. However, if either of you are more comfortable having an attorney present, please do.”

On the way to Janet's room, Elton stopped by Pauline's room. She was on her recliner reading a book.

“How's the book Pauline, any good?” asked Elton.

“I don't even know what I am reading at this point. Just trying to take my mind off poor Janet. I hope nothing bad happened to her. She was such a good friend, so nice.”

“Pauline, can you tell me about finding Janet?”

“I heard Brian and Janet talking in the hall. They were right outside my room. Then Brian went on to his room. I had borrowed a book from Janet and was taking it back to her.”

“Did you hear anything from her room before you went there?”

“No. My hearing is not bad but not what it used to be and I had the local news on the TV. My door was closed and so was Janet's. I came out of my room and knocked on her door. She didn't answer but I knew she was in the room. Her door was not completely closed and when I knocked, the door opened a bit and I saw her on the bed. I thought she was sleeping but it didn't look right. She always rested in that nice reclining chair her son bought for her. Seeing her on the bed was odd. I called to her, but she was so still. I called louder and no reaction. At that point I was quite concerned and went over to her.”

“Did you see any signs of trauma or violence, maybe some disturbance to the room?”

“No, but you have to understand that I was mainly focused on her pulse and breathing. I did not look around the room. Then I called Carol.”

“I've asked Linda and Carol to give us a statement. I think it would be a good idea if you gave us one also. If you like, the three of you can come downtown together and give your statements. You know what? With three of you, let me set it up so you can do it all here. It will be a lot easier on everyone. I'll schedule it with Linda and she can let you know the time."

Elton stopped by Brian's room before going into Janet's room.

"Brian, why don't you come with me to Janet's room. A second set of eyes familiar with the room will be helpful."

When they entered the room Brian said, "You can tell someone's been in the room. Drawers not completely closed, books disturbed, pillow missing from the bed."

"Good observations my friend. You've got a good eye. The pillow is at the lab. On the other side of it the techs found some residue. Maybe vomit, saliva, nasal fluid? They're looking at it now."

"That sounds bad," Brian said.

"Let's follow the evidence and not get ahead of ourselves."

They spent the next hour looking around the room. Brian explained how Janet would always rest in her recliner. She used to joke that beds are for sleeping and recliners are for resting. Elton listened carefully and took notes of their conversation. They headed back to Brian's room as he wanted to brief Elton on the Edsel car. At this point all information had value. Just as they got to Brian's room, Elton had a call on his cell phone.

"Detective Hendricks? This is Doctor Finn at Binghamton General. We have the autopsy report ready for you."

"I'll come by and pick it up. But, Doc, can you cut to the chase and tell me the cause of death."

"Detective Hendricks, Janet Coddington did not die of natural causes. She was suffocated."

Not surprised, new ballgame, thought Elton.

Chapter 8

AFTER PICKING UP THE autopsy report, Elton met with Phil Raimondi back at headquarters.

"It's a murder investigation now Phil."

"I think we saw it coming," said Phil, "now the game changes. What are your thoughts?"

"Well suffocating someone is hard. You just don't put a pillow over the nose and mouth and count to ten. You really have to lean into it. Maybe straddle them and lean in hard with the pillow. It's not a casual act. Sustained pressure for ten minutes or so. Not an easy thing to do. Suffocation murders are usually overplayed in novels and movies. It's a violent act, takes some minutes and requires considerable force. Given the timeline on this between Brian and Pauline, I've the feeling that the person was probably in her room before she arrived. Maybe she surprised the person? Also, Phil, I don't see a resident doing this. Too much of a physical challenge. It was probably someone younger with good upper body strength."

"Employee?" said Phil.

"That would be my first place to look."

Elton continued, "I don't think the security cameras will show us much initially. They have a fairly large staff there and it's an open place in terms of folks walking around. Maybe later we can use the video to confirm a person was in the vicinity of Ms. Coddington's room, but the video probably will not give us any standalone evidence."

"How do you want to start?"

"I'll start with the video to see if anyone was moving quickly through the recorded areas. Maybe under stress, suspicious movements, stuff like that. We know when the attack happened, so I'll get a list of the folks on duty that day."

Phil asked, "Are there multiple entry points to the west wing?"

"Yes, there are exit doors at the end of the wings leading to the parking lot and also halfway down the wing. They are open during the day to allow access from the parking areas as many of the senior living residents have cars."

"So, access points from the lobby and two others from the wing."

"You got it," Elton said.

"Is it possible someone could have come into the place from the outside without going through the lobby?"

"Yes, the doors in the west wing are unlocked from 8 a.m. to 6p.m. However, I think it was someone inside the building. But we'll check it all out."

Phil and Elton discussed the next steps. A lot of information needed to be gathered for the investigation. Names of all the employees, background checks on them, review the video feeds, review the autopsy report, try to find a pattern and look at Janet's background. Was there something there from the past that would account for her death? Seemed like a longshot but in any investigation, all the information has value until you determine that it doesn't.

A few days later, Phil ran into the Broome County District Attorney, Mary Louise Eldridge at the courthouse,

"I see from the newspapers that you have an investigation ongoing from the death over at Edgewood Gardens."

"Sure do Mary Louise. Cause of death was not from natural causes," said Phil.

"Who's your lead detective on the case?"

"Elton Hendricks."

"Good cop. He's thorough."

Phil replied, "That he is and we need that skill set on this case. Elton's a good detective, great future ahead for him. We were lucky to get him."

"Do you need anything from my office?"

"Not at this point, but it might be interesting if Elton had an outside party to confer with as this moves along. Is Brad Petronella still doing work for you?"

"He's on call for the office. Spud and I use him as required. He's not working on anything right now. Please tell Elton he can call him anytime if he wants a third-party input."

"Yikes, two detail guys! I'll pass it on to Elton, it's his call. No pun intended!" They broke off the conversation as Mary Louise was due in court and Phil was late for a meeting.

Back at his office Elton called Rob Coddington. "Mr. Coddington, this is Detective Hendricks. I want to give you an update on the investigation. We have a lot of evidence to go through, so it may be some weeks until we have any definitive information. I can tell you that the autopsy report determined that your mother did not die of natural causes. I will be actively working the case and will keep you posted."

"Oh no! Not my mother! Who would do such a terrible thing? She was a sweet gentle person, never had a bad thing to say about anyone. Why would someone do this to her?

"Mr. Coddington, we'll find out."

"Thanks for calling me. I know it was not an easy one to make."

Janet's funeral was a simple service held at Trinity Memorial Church in Binghamton. Both Rob and Brian delivered moving eulogies. Rob covered the time growing up. Brian the time Janet was with them at Edgewood Gardens. Many fond memories from both men. The service was well attended. Friends from Edgewood Garden, Binghamton and the surrounding area. Janet was buried next to her husband George at Vestal Hills Memorial Park.

Chapter 9

WHEN BRIAN NEXT HOSTED the team managers at Edgewood Gardens, they had made good progress. Using the hockey team as the baseline model proved to be a good choice as there was a lot of equipment and other moving parts. The spreadsheet was divided into sections covering playing equipment such as sticks, pucks, uniforms, protective pads and helmets. Expendable gear such as tee shirts, sweatshirts. Another section for game scores and player game performance. Also sections for game schedules, practices and academic performance. The academic part was very interesting to Brian as it gave him a good look into the thinking of the managers and the role they would play in this area. They had designed a protocol where only three people had access to a player's academic performance, the vice principal for academics, the coach and the team manager. Any contact with a player by the team manager regarding academic performance had to be approved by the coach. The managers were sensitive to privacy concerns the players had and they wanted to respect it. Brian was impressed; they had a clear way forward. The hockey team's spreadsheet had enough complexity to provide a good model for the other spreadsheets. All the students at Binghamton High were issued Chromebooks for regular class and homework. The managers would set up a secure file on their Chromebooks for all the team information.

During one of the breaks, one of the managers asked, "Mr. Reynolds, was someone murdered here?"

"It appears to be the case," replied Brian, "a resident and very good friend of mine died and the police have determined it was not from natural causes. They are actively looking into it now."

"Can we still meet here?"

"Sure we can," replied Brian, "and you don't have to worry about anything. This is a safe environment. I promise you. If anyone has any concerns let's talk about it."

The managers were satisfied that Brian would look after them. Nobody had any immediate objections to continuing at Edgewood Gardens.

"Okay," said Brian, "load up the hockey team data for the next meeting. Don't worry about the names. Just list 10 players starting with Player A to Player J. Then we'll beta test the spreadsheet, clean up the mistakes, and you should be able to load your teams after that."

Carly stopped by Sean's office the next day to brief him on the progress so far. Marcel had been the interface with the coaches, but Carly wanted to make sure Sean was up to speed.

"Coach got a few minutes? I want to update you on our status."

"Sure MC, fire away."

"MC?"

"Manger Carly! What else could it be?"

"Can it just be Carly?"

"Not a problem."

"Well," said Carly, "we're in pretty good shape. We have a baseline model which is the hockey team. I like it because it has lots of stuff in it and will mirror well with football. Brian is a really nice guy and hasn't told us what to design. He wanted us to design it and he would help us implement it. We have good security for the player grades, and the various parts such as equipment and scheduling are broken into logical pieces."

"I think you like it Carly."

"I do Coach and it is so much fun designing this and seeing it come to life. We'll run it off of our school laptops in password protected files. You can access it and so can the vice-principal for academic affairs. Nobody else can get to it without your okay. All the data will be stored on the cloud, so we don't have to worry about hard drives crashing or becoming corrupted. I think Brian is really happy with it and with us. He's always laughing and joking with us and the people at the senior living home are really nice."

Carly stopped for a minute and appeared lost in thought. Finally, she said, "Coach, there was a lady killed over there a few weeks back."

"I know Carly. It was a good friend of Brian's. I spoke with him about it and asked him to be upfront with you guys. There isn't a lot to tell yet as it's under investigation."

"Do you think they will catch the person who did this?"

"I do. I really do, and I'm not just saying this to make you feel safe. Give the police some space to do their job and they'll find the person."

"Who do you think did this?"

"A very bad person, that's all I know at this point. Don't speculate Carly, we don't have any information. All we'll do at this point is develop a lot of off the wall conspiracy theories."

Sean asked, "Question for you, Carly, who is looking after your grades?"

"I guess you've not met my mom and dad. They're hawks."

"Good to know. When we have our team and parents meeting before the first game, please bring them."

"They would love it, thanks."

After the meeting Carly headed off home on the late school bus to fight another round of sexist battles with her two older brothers. Sean went back to his potential roster for the year and wondered about the newbies who would be trying out for the team. You just never know. He was always excited about the hidden potential of the new players. That quiet kid standing on the outside of the circle might be another Tommy

Reynolds. That other lanky kid in the back can run like the wind. Who knows?

Chapter 10

ELTON HAD TWO WHITEBOARDS in his office. Both loaded with information and a to-do list. A neat pile of the statements from Brian, Carol, Linda, and Pauline, Janet's autopsy report, the crime scene report and the coroner's report all on a table next to the whiteboards. Over the past two weeks he had interviewed the staff at Edgewood Gardens. Nothing outstanding from the interviews. The crime scene unit did not turn up anything unusual. They dusted for fingerprints. The dresser and bed table had numerous prints from Janet, staff and friends. All of them had reason to be in the room. The crime did not involve any hard surfaces, so it made things difficult.

Elton asked Brian, "Did Janet have any jewelry or anything else of value?"

"Janet was not a jewelry person. She had some nice pearls and a broach or two. She did have a couple of nice pieces that came from her husband's mother. I think she kept them in a little box in her dresser. You know about George's watch. I know the watch was a Longines. I would guess it was well over $1,000. I don't know about the jewelry; she never wore any of it that I remember other than a diamond ring. She only mentioned the other jewelry once or twice. You could check with Rob. He may know more about it. Maybe put a price on the watch."

"Well, clearly robbery," said Elton, "jewelry and watch are gone."

He continued, "I've contacted the pawn shops and jewelry stores, but we don't have a clear description of the items. I told them to be on the lookout for someone trying to offload jewelry and a watch. We've not given them much to go on. I've a call into Rob to see if he can help."

Rob called back later in the day. He was back in Albany.

"Rob, do you know what kind of watch your father had. The one your mom was always wearing?"

'Yeah, it was a Longines Flagship. I used to joke with dad about it telling him I wanted it. He always said talk to your mother!"

Elton asked, "What did it cost?"

"I don't really know. It was a retirement gift from some clients. You can probably look it up, but I would guess well over $2500, easy."

"What about the jewelry?"

"Mom was not a collector of jewelry. She did have some pieces from Grandma Coddington. I think from the 1920s. Grandma always had nice things and dressed well. It wasn't junk."

Elton felt he had a sense of what happened. Someone stole a watch and jewelry from Janet. She probably caught him in the act. He killed her. Who did this?

Elton remembered Phil saying he could call Brad Petronella over at the DA's office if he wanted to bounce it all off a third party. He called the DA's office and Spud Prono gave him Brad's cell phone number.

"Brad? This is Elton Hendricks. I work for Phil Raimondi in the detective division. Do you have some time to meet with me? I'm working on a case and am at the point where I feel like I'm starting to go round in circles."

"Sure. I remember you. We testified in the Snappy convenience store robbery last year. What are you working on these days?"

"The murder over at Edgewood Gardens."

"That's a sad one. When do you want to meet?"

"Day after tomorrow at 10 a.m.?" asked Elton. "We can meet at my office. I've all the files here and a white board full of notes."

"That's fine, see you then."

When Brad arrived, Elton started out by giving him a comprehensive overview of the case. He went through the police statements, autopsy report, coroner's report, and crime scene report. He also briefed Brad on the physical layout of the building, security cameras, and access points to the west wing.

He finished by saying, "We have a robbery and murder. I don't believe it was anyone outside of Edgewood Gardens. Someone working there did this. Brad, what is driving me crazy at this point is that I can't identify a suspect. There has to be a trail here, but I can't find it. I worry that all I'm going to end up doing is tickling the problem and never get to the bottom of it."

"Hmm, so what I'm hearing is that the crime scene is not conclusive, the video is not specific and neither has any value at this point. Correct?"

"That's right."

Brad continued, "The initial interviews were also inconclusive. Correct?"

"Yes."

"Okay," said Brad, "let's put aside the lady's room, the west wing, and the security video. We can always come back to them but at this point they don't have anything to offer. Let's also put the women aside for now as possible attackers. I think suffocation requires too much strength for an older woman. Not saying it can't be done but you need to have a young lady on the staff, in good shape. Let's put them aside for now."

"There is a young activities director, but she was on vacation the week Ms. Coddington was killed," Elton replied.

"I suggest going back to the male staff and look at them all carefully. Employment history, background check, finances, any priors. Develop a file for each person. Work schedule, job responsibilities, etc. Find out all you can. Most important, develop a matrix of each one's work schedule both days and hours."

"I have a lot of that already, Brad, but maybe not organized in the way you are speaking about."

"I figured you did. Now, there is another aspect that I suggest you look at. Is there a history there for theft? Any kind and any level. I know that theft is not uncommon in senior living centers and nursing homes. Maybe there is a pattern here. When I was coming over to your office, my mindset was a single occurrence of robbery. But I wonder?"

"That's a good point. Many thanks for another set of eyes on this. It really helps. I was getting wrapped around the proverbial axle. Can we stay in touch and maybe meet again as this develops?"

"Yeah, anytime, give me a call."

Chapter 11

BRIAN MET UP WITH BILL and Maggie Wilson at dinner that evening. They had been developing a list of missing items at the home. The search had been wide ranging. Any items, any value, any dates. The plan was to review it all and see what they had in terms of number of items, accuracy of the data and a timeline.

Brian asked Maggie, "Okay Sherlock, what do you have for me?"

"Well" Maggie said, "a lot of data but I'm afraid we really need to vet it for our spreadsheet to have any real value. The data is not always crisp in terms of items, dates, value, you name it. The biggest problem is in the comprehensive care part of the home. The clients are so easily confused."

Bill chimed in, "Maggie's been great with the residents who are in comprehensive care. She's so patient with them and it's really helped. Some have very specific memories of items especially if they were part of their family over a long time. Gifts or recent purchases are difficult. She did a lot better than I thought she would."

"Bill, we also need to mention to Brian that there's probably a disconnect between when the item might have been stolen and when it was noted by the resident."

"Yeah, we assumed that any dates given us were the dates when the item was taken but it's not the case. We may know when it was noted as missing but not necessarily when it was actually taken. We'll will need a column for items that are clearly taken on a specific date and another date for when the item is noted as missing."

"That's interesting," Brian replied, "never really considered it."

Maggie replied, "The dates are much crisper for the senior living residents as you might expect. However, the ones under comprehensive care are not a total loss. I was surprised that some of them wore a particular piece every day as a remembrance of their family history or a particular person. Much like Janet did with George's watch. I think we may be able to see a pattern or trend, but it won't be a straight line to an individual."

"That's okay," said Brian, "let's put it all together and see what we have. What about the value of the items?"

"We need to be careful," said Bill, "you were right when you warned us about this earlier. Value seems to really go up over time!"

"Gentlemen," said Maggie, "let's list value when we can back it up with specific information such as a model, maker, purchase records or provenance. If we can't do that, we'll rely on the best description of the item that we can pull together."

"Good call Maggie. Are you getting any pushback from Linda or any of the staff on this?"

"Not really Brian. Some of the staff might be taking it personally but nothing we can't work around. Linda, the day manager, has been very supportive. She's even given us access to her file on possible thefts. The files go back almost ten years."

"How close are you to finalizing your search?"

Bill replied, "What do you think Maggie? We still have about fifteen people to interview. Two weeks?"

"I think that's realistic."

They finished dinner talking about the spreadsheet and what it would look like. Brian told them that the sheet would not be very complicated in terms of data presented but it had to be carefully annotated. The people providing input to the sheet covered a wide cognitive range and they needed to make sure it was kept in perspective. The date when an item was taken and the date it was noticed as missing was of particular concern to Brian. It could be a few days or many months. They needed to address this in the spreadsheet.

"What about this approach." Brian said, "maybe show the data as category A, B, C? 'A' would be for definitive information and 'C' would be for information not very well backed up. Price, time it went missing and description of the item may not be clear. 'B' would cover items where we have some information but not complete. We may find that category 'A' would provide more of a direct link to a thief and the other categories would be more for backup. This would lend credibility to the study."

"I like it," replied Maggie.

As it seemed to happen a lot these days, they finished up talking about Janet. She was well liked and on everyone's mind.

"Do you have any more information, Brian?"

"Sorry I don't. Detective Hendricks is actively working on it though. I think they're pretty sure it was someone from the home and are concentrating on employees."

"Goodness," Maggie said, "what's the world coming to these days? Rob and kill someone. For what? A few items of some value? Is that all a person's life is worth?"

"I know," said Brian, "makes no sense. What a loss. She was such a good friend. I really miss her."

Brian went back to his room to finish up his current Lee Child book and see if Reacher got all the bad guys. He did! He always did! Reacher was the man! After that, the local news and bed. He needed to prepare for the team managers who would be at the Home after school the next day.

Before he fell asleep Brian was mulling over the spreadsheet that Bill and Maggie were developing. Once finished, they would have far more definitive information about robberies at the home than the police. Detective Hendricks only had access to Linda's file on items that went missing, apparently stolen, and staff interviews. From what

Bill and Maggie said the file was not very comprehensive even though it went back almost ten years. Bill and Maggie would have a better database than the cops. Their database would have time, value, descriptions and be shown in categories for accuracy. Brian made a mental note to get with detective Hendricks when they finished their work. Two weeks? Now that the police were looking primarily at employees this could have real value. He thought to himself, *maybe we can help, in some way to catch the guy who killed Janet?'*

Chapter 12

THE TEAM MANAGERS WERE all in the meeting room when Brian arrived and he was early! Great spirit from the kids. They had bought into the program. Carly was evolving as the go-to person for the group. She was probably the best computer head and was a good communicator. She did not preach to the others. Always respectful and looking for value in their comments. She was with two other managers at a table helping them sort out some computer issues. One of the students she was meeting with, Ray Carmichael, was the baseball team manager.

"Ray, I'm not going to fix your computer," she said, "but I'll tell you how to do it. That way you will be better prepared for the next problem."

"Okay, Carly," said Ray, "let me get my magic fix-it book out and take down some notes." Ray had a small spiral binder notebook filled with all kinds of tips and fixes.

"Well, I guess you've all the bases covered with your notebook."

"I do," said Ray, "and it keeps growing. I'm going to have to go to book two pretty soon."

Brian called the group to order. "Okay, guys, did anyone have any issues loading up the hockey information? Did it make sense to you? Did we miss anything? What do you like and what don't you like? Let me walk around and take a look at your inputs on your screens to make sure we are all in the same room."

Brian was pleased with what he saw. All the spreadsheets were very close in terms of data. Nothing essential was missing.

"Let me go over the basic architecture and rules of engagement for the spreadsheet to make sure we're all together. The spreadsheet will reside on your school laptop under password control. Only you, your coach, and the vice principal will have access to your spreadsheet. When you open the spreadsheet, there will be a listing of areas that apply to all the teams. Even if you don't have to populate an area, all our spreadsheets will all have the same organization and format. That way we have one common software load. Team schedules, practices, equipment, player metrics, game scores, and academics. The biggest difference between your spreadsheets will be equipment. As you can see, hockey is busy. Once you access the home page on the spreadsheet, you click on a particular area and it opens up. You make the call on frequency of updating but I strongly suggest you do it every day. Once the season starts, it will be busy. If you get behind, we have big problems. You guys are the source now so make sure you are up to date. Okay?"

Ray asked, "what if my computer is stolen or broken?"

"You've got a problem with the school. But it's a hardware problem. All our spreadsheet data will be stored on the cloud. So, get on another computer, access your school account then open up the team spreadsheet and away you go."

Brian continued, "Some of the coaches will be tuned into this more than others. You got to sell the package. Plan on meeting with your coach and let him see how you use the system."

Marcel Argentaru, the hockey coach, was at the meeting. "I think it will be an easy sell. When we talked about this at our coaches meeting, everyone was in agreement. If you do get some pushback, let me know and I will get with Coach Sean and we will run interference for you."

"What's next, Brian?" Carly asked.

"Well, I'm going to change gears on you a bit. I had thought that each one of you would populate your spreadsheets and then we would meet again to sort it all out. However, you guys have moved along a lot faster than I anticipated. Your data inputs for the hockey team are very good. So much so that Marcel and his manager Bobby Miller get a free ride. Their spreadsheet is launched! I'd like to do the following: I've access to all of your spreadsheets and will have until the school year ends. Given the good progress you've made, you populate your team spreadsheets and I'll review them. Just send me an email telling me you're ready to review the work. We can do all this online and it will get us up and running and set the standard for how we'll interface during the season. We still may want to meet a couple of times during the school year as a group to see how it's all going. I'd also like a group meeting before Summer break to do a summary report for Coaches Sean and Marcel. One final thought: Even if your sport does not start until Spring, like track and field or baseball, don't wait on it. Start populating your spreadsheets now and we'll finalize them as we get closer to your season. Also, talk to the other managers to see what their experiences are. Everyone on board?"

"You can play us Coach, we got game!" exclaimed Bobby Miller.

Chapter 13

WHEN BRIAN GOT BACK to his room, there was a call from Johnny Forman waiting for him. He called back and found him still at work.

"Don't you ever stop working, Johnny? It's almost 6 o'clock."

"Got to get this car out, promised a guy."

"Go slow, Johnny, there's life outside of the shop."

"I know, Brian, but the work comes in spurts and if you take it in then you've got to deliver. Anyway, enough of that. I have some info on the Edsel for you and we need to talk about what the family wants to do especially after what happened to Ms. Coddington."

"Okay, where are we?"

"The charge of scoping out the job was $380. Ms. Coddington gave me $500 so, the Coddington's have $120 coming back or they can apply it to the restoration if they decide to go forward with it."

"How much will the restoration cost?"

"$4,900. The big driver is the new convertible top. It's a custom-made job and priced out at $1,500. I also had a guy I work with on Upper Front Street give me a quote for doing the detail work on the inside of the car. He's very good. I've used him before. Brian, what I'm telling you now is what I know at this time. There may be some surprises once I get going. The car has been in storage since Christ was a corporal so there may be some other issues. I won't know for sure until I start the work. But, at this point I don't see anything. However, I suggest you tell the Coddington's to plan on $6,000."

"I need to call her son Rob and see what he wants to do. I don't believe he has any interest in keeping the car and your estimate for the refurb is much better than I anticipated. I think he'll want to have the work done. I'll call him and come right back to you."

"No panic, Brian, I have space for the car here."

Brian called Rob at home in Albany. He reviewed John Forman's evaluation of the job. Rob was not an antique car guy. Brian did not expect him to embrace the next steps.

"Thanks for the update on the car. What do you think I should do? I really don't have much interest in dragging it around to car shows to build up its credentials and interest. I want to sell it but candidly don't want to put a lot of time into it."

"Rob, for the next steps, you don't have to do anything at this point other than fund John 50% of the cost of the refurbishment to purchase the parts. I don't think the car will be finished for three months or so. John does not want to start the job until he has all the parts in hand. So other than throwing $2500 at the car now you don't have to cross any other bridges."

"I'll go ahead with the refurbishment Brian. It seems like the obvious choice. I guess I'm thinking about the nausea of selling it after the work is done."

Brian replied," I wouldn't worry about any of that now, Rob. Get the car in good selling shape and sort the rest out when you have to. I think John would let you keep the car at his shop and he could broker any sale. If you want the car in Albany, we hire a truck and bring it up to you. We'll need to develop a marketing plan to sell the car once the refurb is finished but that's not a big effort. I've the feeling that once the word is out that another 1960 Edsel Ranger has been found you'll get a lot of interest. Don't forget there are only 25 of them left and this car is in mint condition. It's a show stopper. This is like finding a lost Rembrandt!"

"You're right Brian. Would you call John and tell him the checks in the mail."

After the call Brian went to the dining room looking for Bill and Maggie but they had gone out for the evening. When he got back to his room, he decided to call Tommy. He had not talked with his son in a while, and it was always good to hear his voice.

"Tommy, it's your father calling with some life altering advice for you!"

"Pop! I could not have lasted another day without some guidance. What should I do oh wise one?"

"Give all your money to your father and let him invest it in timeshares!"

"Oh, sure! Other than that Pop, what's up?"

"Oh, nothing special, just missed your voice and wanted to update you on stuff here."

Brian told Tommy of the progress with the high school kids on the spreadsheets and how they had them ready to launch. It had turned out much better than he imagined. The kids were great to be around and they had taken over the senior living center when they had their meetings. The residents looked forward to seeing them at the home.

"Pop, what's going on with the Edsel?"

"It's a cream puff and Janet's son is okay with refurbishing it. No clear road on how to sell it at this point but it's not a big problem. Janet and I were going to shop it around some antique car shows but Rob has no interest in doing that. So, we'll develop a market for it. The car is solid; I don't think we'll have a problem."

Tommy asked about any developments regarding Janet Coddington.

"I'm not read into the investigation as you can imagine. Elton calls me with questions and sometimes asks my opinion on some things, I think he is concentrating on male employees. He did tell me he met with a guy named Brad Petronella at the DA's office. Elton wanted a third-party set of eyes to look at the case."

"I know Brad," Tommy said, "I was involved with him awhile back regarding a young lad who went missing years ago in Scranton. Brad pieced it all together. Good guy."

"It made the papers here. Coach McCarthy was part of it also."

"That's right."

"Anyway, I think Elton is trying to match the thefts in the home over the years with employment histories. I don't think he has much to go on because the files here on thefts are not comprehensive at all."

"Pop, what are you not telling me?" How do you know about the files on theft at the home? What else do you have in play?"

"Don't worry, Tommy, I'm not running a rogue operation! It's all very interesting. Before Janet was killed, I was having dinner with her and another couple who live here. We had just started developing the matrix for the team managers. I was telling them, that is Janet, Maggie, and Bill, about the project and how we were using a spreadsheet to capture the data. Maggie said that we should develop something like that to capture all the theft in the home over the years. It's never all reported, usually forgotten, and basically sporadic in terms of when it happens. But over time it tells a story. Bill and Maggie volunteered to collect the data from the senior living residents and also the folks under comprehensive care. We have about two more weeks of work left and then should have something to show. The day manager, Linda, is supportive of this effort and let us look at her files. That's how I know they're not very good."

"I've never heard of anything like that," said Tommy. "We get cases coming through here about care home theft but usually don't have enough evidence to go to trial. No trail, care home staff change jobs and there is never a consistent pattern we can tie to an individual. We know it happens but can't get many convictions."

"I'll send you a copy of our spreadsheet when we finish, assuming it tells a story."

Tommy replied, "Make sure you give this to Elton also, it could be a game changer Pop."

"I'll do it Tommy. I want to see the end product first; it could be a bunch of extraneous information."

"That's possible, Pop, but it's more than Elton has now and it may give him a track to follow and if it's really good, bingo!"

"Okay, now, Tommy; about those timeshares?"

"I'll be up your way next week and will bring a big bag of money to launch your new investment venture!"

"My boy! The best!"

"Good night Pop."

Chapter 14

SEAN HELD A TEAM MEETING to introduce Carly to them and also review the practice and game schedules. This was the time to set the tone for the season and also define team goals. Their first game was with Elmira High and Sean was worried about it. Word was they have a very good team. They were always well coached. Sean would have preferred to play them at mid-season, but the conference schedule and outside conference games were out of his control. You lived with the published schedule. The team needed to be ready to play. No tune- up games this year.

The team was happy to have Carly as the manager. She was going into her junior year and knew many of them. Her computer skills were well known at the school. Having two older brothers was an asset for Carly. She was not intimidated by the guys.

After the meeting ended, Carly was walking out to catch the late school bus. DeShawn Wilkins caught up with her.

"Carly, you headed for the bus?"

"Yeah. You?"

"Yup. If I miss this bus it takes forever on the Broome County buses. I would have to transfer at the Oakdale Mall to get home."

Carly asked, "What's your course load look like this year?"

"Whatever. I take what comes down on the schedule. I'm going to play NFL football anyway. Play Division 1 football and then move on to the NFL."

"That's it? That's the game plan?"

"Yeah. I know what I'm doing."

Carly did not press DeShawn any further on his career plans but found it troubling. So many kids dream of a life in pro-sports but the window for entry is so small. She would talk to Coach McCarthy about this tomorrow.

Sean usually taught three classes. This year he was teaching Geometry, Algebra 2 and AP Math. Her last class of the day was AP Math with the coach, so it was easy to catch him when class ended.

"Coach, can we talk for a few minutes?"

"Sure, let's sit in the classroom, it's quiet now."

Carly went over the conversation with DeShawn and her concerns about the reality of his plan. She also bought up the point that many of the other players were talking about Division 1 and the NFL. She told the coach that most of these guys were in la-la land and headed for a big letdown.

"Well, Carly," said Sean, "you'll hear lots of talk like that. I know most of the guys talk a big game but know it won't happen. I don't want to shut down a dream and as the season progresses most of them see where they stack up playing against the other teams and especially when they come up against a star player."

"I understand, Coach, but what worries me is that some of these guys will sacrifice academics chasing this dream. Once reality sets in it may be too late and they have really hurt themselves looking ahead to college."

"You're right, Carly," replied the coach, "making it in professional sports is so hard. Very few ever get there. I've been here over twenty-five years and we've had only one guy make it to the NFL. Tommy Reynolds. You've probably seen his picture and history in the lobby. I think we also had a couple of baseball players and one basketball player. And that's after twenty-five years! A lot of guys have gone through our system in that time."

"Coach, Tommy's father is Brian Reynolds who is helping us with the spreadsheets. Do you think he could get Tommy to talk to all the athletes? Men and women?"

"Yeah, we can do that. I usually get a call from Tommy when he's in town to see Brian. I'm sure he would be happy to talk to the players. I'll call Brian. We'll make it happen."

Sean called Brian that night. He needed to speak with him about the spreadsheets. The usual stuff, progress, problems, and next steps. After they finished up on business, he asked Brian about having Tommy speak with all the team players about academics and professional sports.

"Brian said, "Tommy will be in town late next week. I can ask him to meet with the kids then. I'm sure he'll do it."

"Okay, Brian, thanks. By the way, it was Carly's idea and she's spot on with the issue."

Brian confirmed the meeting with Tommy and Sean reserved the school auditorium for the talk. It was a good thing he reserved the auditorium. Once the word got out that Tommy Reynolds would be speaking at the school, the teachers and many of the students wanted in on the talk. It was a full house. All the seats taken and students standing along the walls on the outside aisles.

Mr. Envers, the school principal, introduced Tommy to a loud round of applause. Tommy was mostly remembered as an NFL player, but he still had some school records that still stood. It was clear from the beginning that Tommy was not going to preach to the audience. After the introduction, he looked over the audience then walked off the stage and went up and down the middle aisle of the auditorium. He did not say anything, just looked at the kids as he walked past. Nobody knew what he was doing, and there was a lot of murmuring throughout the audience. Sean thought to himself, *Tommy, you are going to own this audience, you really got their attention.*

Tommy returned to the stage and started his talk with a question. "Let's say I gave each of you $100 and we all go to the track at Tioga Downs. You have to bet it all on one horse race. How would you bet? Would you bet on a 40-1 longshot? The favorite at 2-1? A combination of win, place, show bets? The Trifecta? I don't know, but one thing I am pretty sure about is that nobody is going to bet $100 on a 40-1 long-shot. Why? Simple! It's not my best chance of winning. You need to think of your future in the same context. What is my best chance of winning? Is it sports? Is it a business career? Public service? The point is that you don't put your money, or let me say it, your future, on a long shot. Always have a Plan B and maybe even Plan C!

Sean looked around the audience. Tommy really had their attention. They were focused on him for sure.

Tommy continued, "Now, this is really important. At this point in your life nothing is impossible. You can't dream big enough. Dream big, think big! But, I just told you to have a Plan B and maybe a Plan C. Am I telling you to plan on failure? No, not at all. It all comes down to how you put the package together. Look, if you put all your eggs in the sports basket and it does not work out for whatever reason, you're screwed. No fall back, no options. But, if you make your academics an integral part of the sports package, you have options. Options, that's the name of the game. That's what an education gives you. Options! You've got to be smart. Only 2% of athletes across the NCAA end up in professional sports. Can you be one of the 2%? Damn right you can, and you should work hard towards that goal. But, if you don't make the cut, you've got options! Now, not everyone here plays sports, but the strategy applies to us all. We have to think about our lives in terms of changing circumstances. Nothing is permanent. The only constant is change! Plan for this. Make sure you can adapt and move on. It's a great ride, embrace it.

Tommy then got more personal about his life. "Look, I'm a lucky guy. I came out of Binghamton High with a full ride to Syracuse.

Playing Division 1 football is sort of a game by game experience. If you get hurt, then you're gone. It's that simple. I had Syracuse back up my scholarship to cover any career ending injuries. I also got them to fill in my missed classes and labs with Summer school. Finally, assuming my grades were adequate, they promised me a place in the law school. I would have gone right from undergraduate to law school, but when I got drafted by the NFL, they agreed to let me attend law school off season and online. Took seven years. The law was where I wanted to end up and that was my game plan. Now, if Division 1 football is high risk, the NFL is super high risk. Plan B was always in play. And that's the message today. Friends, life is full of surprises, make sure you have a good foundation and plan B! Maybe Plan C, too! Now, if I had to leave you today with one word, what would it be? Options, my friends, options!"

Tommy got a standing ovation. Sean teared up and was glad nobody saw him. The coach with tears? Can't happen! Tommy spent the next hour answering questions. It was surprising how many of the questions were about being a prosecutor in the Attorney General's office. Tommy finished up by telling the kids to send him an email at the AG's office if they had any other questions.

After that Sean, Tommy, and Brian went out to dinner at Lampys in Endicott and talked about the football days and listened to Tommy's great stories about the NFL. Brian and Sean knew he helped out a lot of his NFL friends who had financial, insurance, and medical issues but he never spoke about it.

Chapter 15

BRIAN MET UP WITH BILL and Maggie who had finished the data gathering part of the exercise. They divided the data into the A-B-C. categories and populated the spreadsheet. Category A items had complete data. Date, description, and value. Category B items had incomplete data, missing maybe one or two elements. Category C items did not have enough data to conclusively identify them. The spreadsheet certainly showed a pervasive picture of theft. Consistently, over the years, residents were reporting items missing. As expected, the majority of the reports of Category A items came from the senior living residents. But the category A items from the comprehensive care residents were actually better than expected. It was pretty much centered around items that were worn on a daily basis. They were immediately missed. Category C didn't have much value for either group at the home as the information was too vague. Category B provided more credibility to the spreadsheet by showing that something was happening but couldn't be fully documented at the time.

"Let's review this again tomorrow to make sure we have the data placed in the proper categories," suggested Brian, "then we can sit down with Linda and show her the results."

Maggie replied, "Okay, good call, what about showing this to Detective Hendricks?"

"I'll call him this afternoon. I think you two should be part of the meeting as you know much more about the data and can fill in any holes."

Brian called Elton that afternoon.

"Good afternoon, Elton, this is Brian over at Edgewood Gardens."

"Hi, Brian, nice to hear your voice. What can I do for you?"

"Can we meet here at the home? Two of our residents have developed a database regarding past thefts here over the years, and I think you should take a look at it. It's comprehensive and may have some value in your investigation."

"Sounds good. I've gone through the manager's file, and talked to the staff about this. It wasn't conclusive at all."

"I know. Bill and Maggie, who collected the data, also reviewed Linda's file and came to the same conclusion."

"Do you mean that their data is better?"

"Much better."

"That's great! I'm in court in the morning. Can we meet after lunch, say 2 p.m.?"

"That will work. We'll have some fresh coffee waiting for you."

"Thanks, no snacks though. Everything I eat these days I end up sitting on!"

Brian reserved one of the small meeting rooms at the home. He did not want to cause any concern among the residents with the police being at the home. Everyone knew there was an active investigation ongoing, and any police presence at the home fueled speculation. They met in a small room off the lobby. Brian introduced Bill and Maggie and asked them to brief Elton on their research.

"Detective Hendricks," said Maggie," I think the best way to do this is to start with our strategy in developing the spreadsheet and then get into the data."

"That's fine, Ms. Wilson. Please call me Elton."

"Sure, and it's Bill and Maggie."

"As we got into the data gathering, we quickly found that we were dealing with varying levels of credible information. Some good with dates, purchase receipts, names, etc. Others, not so good, and many of the older ones vague. Also, we found that some of the data could be tied to a specific date of a theft and others were dates when the resident noticed it was missing. As you can see a lot of information that does not fit very well into a single category. Brian broke the code on this when he suggested that we put the data into three categories. That is A, B and C. A having the best documentation. B having some documentation but not complete and C for all the items lost in someone's memory and lacking good backup. Once we did that, we got a better picture of what happened over time."

Bill continued, "We don't have access to employment records, so we can't match anything to a person. But we do have a good history of possible thefts now and a lot of dates."

"I'm at a loss for words," said Elton, "this is a first-class job of data gathering and analysis. I'm impressed, really impressed! I have the employment records and can start matching it to your data. Maybe we can get closer to the killer."

"That's a hard word to hear," said Brian. "Killer! It's awful."

Elton took the spreadsheet back to his office and started mapping the data to employment records. He decided to start only with category A items as they all had dates. Most dates were when the item was stolen, so he had good metrics. He only looked at current male employees at this point. He was able to match two men to the timeline for thefts. Both of them fit a period of time when the thefts were more numerous. One was the maintenance manager and the other was a cook. Both had been employed over five years at the home. But when he looked at the photos of them in their personnel files, he remembered them from the initial interviews with the staff. They were both older and overweight. Would they have had the mobility and physical strength to suffocate a healthy woman and leave her room rapidly?

Then he thought he should look at past employees. The turnover of staff was a lot more frequent than he expected. He decided to ask Linda for a list of people who had worked there in the past and left for other employment or were let go.

Elton was more interested in longer term employees. The list Linda gave him was not very long. He immediately noticed the profile of a man who worked there for over ten years and had recently left to work in Albany. He left two days after Janet was killed! Why did he leave after ten years? So close to Janet's murder. Was there a connection?

He decided to check in with Brad and go over the case status before he took the next steps. The new data opened up a lot of leads, and he wanted to get some outside eyes on it to make sure he was headed in the right direction. He also asked Lt. Raimondi to join the meeting. The three men met in Elton's office the next day.

"Guys let me take you through the investigation to date. I think we may have caught a break and I want to have your thoughts before I move on it."

Elton took them through the investigation of thefts and trying to tie it to employment records.

Brad asked, "Are you operating under the premise that Janet's death was part of a robbery?"

"Yes, it's the only motive we can uncover. She didn't have any financial troubles, threats, or anything outside of the home. Her watch was taken as well as some family heirloom jewelry which she kept in her dresser. My opinion is that it was a robbery gone bad."

"I agree," said Phil, "it's the only track that makes sense."

"Yeah, you're right," Brad replied, "anything else would be a hope and a prayer."

Elton continued, "Brian and two other residents have developed a spreadsheet that addresses the thefts over the years. It's far more comprehensive than any records that the home has on file. Also, they have broken it down into three categories to show how well the theft is documented. I have a copy of the spreadsheet, take a look."

Phil and Brad spent the next half hour pouring over the spreadsheet.

"Yikes," Brad exclaimed, "this is really good, I have to tell Mary Louise over at the DA's office about this. We need them to help us out!"

"I've got first dibs, Elton found them!" exclaimed Phil.

Elton continued the discussion of the data by explaining that he had mapped three employees to a time when thefts were more ongoing. Of the three, two were unlikely because of their physical condition and one had recently left the home for other work. It was curious that it was two days after Janet was killed.

Everyone was quiet for a short time. Each lost in their thoughts.

Brad broke the silence. "Elton, this shows real promise. Clearly, the person who left shortly after Janet was killed is very interesting. I also think we need to do some more analysis of the spreadsheet. Now, I'm not a spreadsheet guy, but from my experience with them they can be sliced and diced in many directions and levels. For example, I would get a theft and work timeline for each person of interest on a standalone basis. Name, employment date, and thefts. Each one separate. It will give us a lot more focus. Also, maybe go back and ask Brian to look at the spreadsheet with a detective's eyes. What do I need to know? What can the spreadsheet tell me? There is probably more information to be gained from it."

Phil responded, "Good call, Brad, makes sense."

Elton joined in the conversation, "I want to first run down the guy who left shortly after Janet was killed. In my book, he's a person of interest now."

"You're right," said Brad, "let's not get lost in data and let a potential bad guy get away."

Chapter 16

THE EMPLOYEE WHO LEFT shortly after Janet was killed was William Jenkins. He'd been with the home over ten years in an administrative capacity. He was well liked by the residents, and over the years, got to know many of them by their first names. Elton met with Linda to review his situation.

"Linda, why did he leave?"

"He told me his mother up in Albany, was not doing well and he needed to be near her."

"Is he employed in another care home?"

"Yes, it's a county home, and I believe his mother is a resident there too."

"Did he give you notice that he was leaving?"

"Well, yes and no."

"How so?"

Janet replied, "I knew his mother was not doing well, and we even talked of bringing her here, but she was long established in Albany. Bill thought it would be a difficult adjustment bringing her to Binghamton."

"So, you knew it was coming?"

"I did but it happened quickly. Two days' notice actually."

Elton felt that he needed to speak with Bill Jenkins. He contacted him in Albany and set up a meeting. *Always a nice drive to Albany* thought Elton. I-88 was never crowded and it was pretty much a country drive. Two hours northeast of Binghamton. Coffee stop in

Oneonta going up and coming back. Elton met up with Bill around 11 o'clock.

"The dining room here is pretty good; you can get a sandwich when we finish if you want. Save a fast-food stop on the road."

"Thanks Mr. Jenkins, I'll do that."

Elton explained that he was still investigating the Janet Coddington killing and hoped he could fill in some holes. He did not tell him he was a person of interest. He wanted to keep the conversation as open as possible at this point.

"I understand you worked at Edgewood Gardens for over ten years Mr. Jenkins."

"I did indeed. Hired on right out of the Army."

"Linda at Edgewood Gardens told me you came to Albany to be near your mother."

"That's correct. She was a senior living resident here but now is in comprehensive care. She's declining rapidly, and I am not sure how much time she has left. It all came on so quickly. When I was making arrangements to have her transferred to comprehensive care, I was approached by the management here about a position that had just opened up. I wanted to be near my mom, and working at the same care facility was a great opportunity. So, I jumped at the job and here I am."

"Do you have the same situation here regarding theft from residents?"

"Unfortunately, it comes with the territory, I think. We try to tell the residents to not keep anything of value in their rooms. But that's hard to do. Jewelry, mementos, things like that are part of their life. You can't just put them away in another place. I've always been very careful with Mom's pieces even though we don't have anything of real value. In fact, I have some of her jewelry here in my desk drawer. I make it available for her, but keep it here."

Bill opened his bottom drawer to show Elton a cup with some pieces of jewelry in it.

"I guess we won't break the bank, but it's important to Mom."

Elton asked, "What about Edgewood Gardens?"

"Well", Bill said, "the residents there are wealthier. We are a county nursing home here, and many of our residents don't have a lot of wealth. Edgewood Gardens is a private operation. I don't know if there is more theft there than here. I can say that the value of their possessions are probably higher there."

"What is your experience with theft in these places?"

Bill replied, "Usually someone working there. Over the years we have suspected an individual of theft, but it is so hard to conclusively prove they did it. Sometimes they know we are looking at them and move on to another care home."

"Do you think that it was someone from Edgewood Gardens who killed Janet?"

"Detective Hendricks, I don't know anything about the case other than what I've read in the papers and some TV news. However, if I were a betting man, I would bet on it being someone from the home. An outside robbery makes no sense to me. The person would have to know their way around the home and the target room. An outside person just doesn't fit.

Janet was a charming person. She used to poke her head into my office and say the funniest things like, Bill are you sure you're working hard? I'll be watching you! She was a lovely lady."

On paper Bill Jenkins had looked to be a person of interest. After meeting with him, Elton ruled him out. He still had a background investigation to complete, but at this point Bill did not seem to merit any further investigation. He seemed genuine, and nothing led Elton to think he knew more than what had been published about the death. He had not mentioned any specific items stolen from Janet's room. That information was withheld from the residents. As he did not mention any items that were in Janet's room, Elton felt he was not involved. Still, he would follow up on his movements.

On the way back to Binghamton Elton thought, *Okay let's look at the other guys and dig a bit deeper into the spreadsheet with Brian. Maybe a different look at the data would help.* When he got back to the office, he checked in with Phil to update him on the Albany trip and called Brian and set up a meeting for the next day at the home. Phil could sense Elton's frustration with the progress on the case.

"Elton, I wish I could offer some help. This is a real slog, and it just seems to go on and on."

"I know, Phil. All we can do is keep our heads down and keep working the information. I thought we caught a break with Bill Jenkins, but it looks like there's nothing there. I have to finish up his background investigation but do not expect anything new. I'm going to see Brian tomorrow and see what his thoughts are on analyzing the data."

Chapter 17

RATHER THAN REVIEW the spreadsheet on hard copy, Brian had it open on his laptop.

"I can show you the system capability much easier this way."

Elton explained that Bill Jenkins was not in play anymore and that they just take a look at the two other employees. He asked Brian to break out the two on separate headings and tie it to their employment history and frequency of thefts. There might be something there isolating each person that showed a more dramatic picture of employment history and thefts, but it did not tie them to anything other than being employed there at that time. Purely circumstantial. Elton had interviewed them earlier when he'd seen all the staff and would do so again showing them the printout to see if there was any reaction.

"Brian, tell me more about the spreadsheet in terms of different presentations."

"Sure. You can display the data in many ways and formats. It's very powerful and allows data to be manipulated. Look at this. We can take all the dates we have in numerical form and show them as calendar days."

Brian went into the spreadsheet and changed all the numerical dates to calendar days. Elton jumped up and almost fell into the screen.

"Can you only show me Category A for the last ten years?"

"Sure, here you go."

"Holy shit!" Look at that, Brian!"

"Whoa, lots of Tuesdays and Thursdays. What's going on here?" asked Brian.

"I'm not sure yet," Elton replied, "but I think our field of inquiry just opened up. I find it hard to believe an employee would only steal on Tuesday and Thursday, it makes no sense. But a service provider? Let's speak with Linda."

Linda came down to Brian's room with her files on service providers.

"We have service providers for daily maintenance, building cleaning, lawn and garden, security equipment, and outside grounds, such as parking lot maintenance and snow plowing. Is this what you are looking for?"

Elton replied, "I'm interested in any service that would consistently be here on Tuesdays and Thursdays. Year after year."

"We let our service contracts for a two-year period and then put them out for rebid. That's a corporate regulation. So, I'm not sure we've had any of these companies under contract for an extended period of time. They win one time, lose the next, and win again the following time. Sort of like musical chairs."

"There has to be a trail here." said Elton, "who else?"

"That's it for our service providers. I may have missed one, but I don't think so."

"What about Jerry Monroe?", asked Brian. "He's been coming here for as long as I've been here. I see him on and off all the time."

"He's a physical therapist on corporate staff," said Linda, "supports our three homes in this area of the state."

"What days?" asked Elton.

"Tuesday and Thursday," replied Linda.

"Brian, what day was Janet killed on?"

"Thursday."

"Linda, how long has Jerry been coming here?"

"I've been here almost fifteen years, and he was coming here when I started."

"Brian! What's wrong with you? Are you okay? Are you sick?" asked Linda.

Brian was clearly shaken and had started to sweat.

"I've only just remembered! Janet had an appointment with Jerry when I dropped her off at her room that day. She had an old elbow injury. Years back she fell on her elbow during a tennis match. I don't think she broke anything but with age, the elbow was becoming arthritic and Jerry was helping her with exercises and manipulation. When it would flare up, she'd call him."

"Linda, where did Jerry usually provide treatment?"

"Usually in the resident's room. It was a privacy issue. Jerry had a portable massage table that he would bring to his appointments."

"Okay," Elton said, "this conversation stays in this room. No discussion with anyone. I need to get with Lt. Raimondi and sort out the next steps. It's really important that you don't talk about this, not even among yourselves. Can you do it?"

Linda and Brian agreed, and Elton felt they could be trusted to not talk about the new information. When Elton got back to the office, he met with Phil.

"Finally, Phil, I think we are closing in on this! Once we displayed the numerical dates as days of the week, we saw a distinct pattern. Tuesday and Thursday over a very long period. We were able to match it to a physical therapist who is a corporate employee. Name is Jerry Monroe. He supports their three nursing homes in this part of the state. Janet was killed on a Thursday and he had an appointment with her late in the afternoon that day!"

"Yes! Finally, a pattern and a good fit," said Phil.

"Phil, I want to pick him up at Edgewood Gardens tomorrow and take him in for questioning. In parallel, I want to execute a search warrant. That way we have him out of his home so we get a better look. I think we have grounds for a warrant."

"We should be okay. I'll get with Judge Richards right away. I'll go with the search team and you handle the interview with Jerry."

Chapter 18

ELTON APPROACHED JERRY the next day as he was getting out of his car at Edgewood Gardens. He was about average height, but with broad shoulders and thick arms. He obviously worked out.

"Mr. Monroe, I'm Detective Hendricks from the Binghamton Police Department. I would like to ask you some questions regarding Janet Coddington. It's easier if we do this at my office downtown."

"I don't have to come with you. I won't talk to anyone from the police without a lawyer."

"First off Mr. Monroe, you do have to come with me. Second, if you want a lawyer present, you can have one. I suggest you call an attorney if you have one, and have the lawyer meet us downtown."

Jerry had no choice but to go with Elton. His only option was to retain a lawyer for the interview.

"I'll follow you in my car," said Jerry.

"No, you'll ride with Officer Miller and me. We can drive you back here when we finish the interview."

As they were going to Elton's office, Phil and his team were at Jerry's house with a search warrant. Jerry's wife was caught by surprise and attempted to stop the search. However, she had no grounds and had to let the team into the house.

"Ms. Monroe, why don't you sit over there on the coach and let us get on with our work. We won't disrespect your property."

"Why are you here? What have we done? I want to speak with my husband!"

"He's downtown in our office being interviewed."

"What's happening?" What did he do?"

Phil said, "We can talk about all of that later."

Back at police headquarters, Jerry was put in a nondescript interview room. Light green and gray walls with a large mirror on one wall. He thought it must be a one way mirror you see on TV and in the movies. Elton let him sit there for thirty minutes or so. He wanted to let him think about what was happening and also give his lawyer time to arrive. When his lawyer arrived, they began the interview. Elton started out by telling the parties that the interview was being recorded, and they could have a copy of the tape if they wanted it. Elton asked Officer Miller to stay in the room with him.

Elton went through Jerry's background, employment history, and role with the company. Then he started to drill down on the issues.

"Jerry, do I understand that you always worked at Edgewood Gardens on Tuesday and Thursday?"

"Yes, I try to have a predictable schedule so the residents know when I will be there."

"You've been doing this for a long time, I see."

"Yeah."

"Was Janet Coddington a client of yours?"

"On and off," said Jerry, "she had an elbow problem and it would act up now and then."

"Did she have an appointment with you on the Thursday she was killed?"

"I don't remember. That was a couple of months ago."

"Well, I do, and here is your schedule for that week."

"Did you see her that day?"

"I don't remember."

Elton pressed, "Come on, Jerry, you can do better than that. Did you see her?"

"Detective," said the lawyer," he doesn't have to answer your questions and your tone is unacceptable. You're badgering my client."

"Okay," Elton said repeating the question in a non-confrontational manner, "Mr. Monroe did you have an appointment with Janet Coddington on that Thursday."

"I guess so."

"Did you meet with her?"

"I'm not sure."

Jerry was trying to evade the answer, but Elton was taking away his maneuvering room. Jerry was probably not aware that Pauline had come to Janet's room shortly after she returned. Just enough time for Jerry to kill Janet and get away. Elton thought Jerry must have come within a heartbeat of being spotted by Pauline.

"Take your time, Jerry. It seems that you had an appointment with her. You must have been with her for some amount of time."

"Oh yeah, I remember," replied Jerry, "we met briefly and rescheduled as I had a conflict with another client."

"Who was the other client Mr. Monroe? I'll need to verify the person's appointment. I don't see anything here in the master schedule from the home."

Jerry replied, "I don't remember offhand. I'll come back to you."

"Okay," Elton said, "but you were with her for some period of time at 4 o'clock or so."

"I guess so."

"Well, Mr. Monroe," replied Elton, "her next-door neighbor Pauline, heard Janet enter her room after talking in the hall with Brian Reynolds. Less than twenty minutes later she went to see Janet and she was dead. Now, you just admitted to me that you were with her at that time."

Jerry was getting agitated and said he wanted to take a break and talk with his lawyer. Elton could not deny them the time and agreed to break for fifteen minutes. As Elton and Officer Miller were leaving the interview room, Phil called.

"We found the Longines!"

"Are you sure?"

"Hell yes," cried Phil, "Longines Flagship and it was engraved on the back. George's name. Also, some jewelry that we want Rob to look at. Maybe he can recognize some of the pieces. It even gets better. Jerry's wife had a nice ring on when we first arrived at the house. When we finished, she had taken it off and tried to hide in the back of a couch cushion. One of our officers saw this. She knew what was going on."

When Jerry came back into the interview room Elton said, "Jerry, we executed a search warrant at your house. In the process, we found a Longines Flagship watch with an engraving on the back to George Coddington. We also found some jewelry. We have taken it and will ask Rob Coddington to take a look at it to see if he can match it to his mom's jewelry. Jerry, I'm placing you under arrest for the murder of Janet Coddington. Before I go any further, let me read you your Miranda rights."

Jerry was arrested and booked into the Broome County jail. Two officers went back to Jerry's house and arrested his wife as an accomplice.

Jerry called Rob that afternoon. "Rob, we made an arrest this afternoon."

"Oh my God!" said Rob, "who was it?"

"A guy who worked for Edgewood Gardens as a physical therapist. We can go into the details later. I need you to come down here tomorrow and take a look at a watch and some jewelry we recovered from a search. We are very comfortable with what we have but I would like you to look at it all."

"Sure, what time?"

"Ten o'clock works. I'm also going to ask Brian to take a look at it also as he may have some memory of it."

When they finished Elton called Brian and gave him the news. It was a great relief to Brian that the case had been solved. It had impacted the day to day life at the home. Now they could move on. Janet would always be missed. She was one of the shining lights at the home.

"It's quite a surprise. I've seen that guy around a lot over the years," said Brian, "nice friendly guy."

Elton replied, "What did your mother say? Don't judge a book by its cover!"

"Guess mom's right."

"Brian, I have Rob coming here tomorrow to look at some recovered items. Watch and jewelry. I think you should also take a look at it and see if you can identify any of it."

"I think I would remember the watch as it had a distinctive alligator band."

Brian called Rob that evening and they went over all the events of the past days. Rob asked Brian to go to Janet's room and bring her photo album to Elton's office. There were a lot of old family pictures. Maybe some of Grandma Coddington would show her wearing her jewelry. Worth a try.

Chapter 19

WHEN THEY ARRIVED AT Elton's office Brian looked at the watch. "That's the band. I can't say I ever saw Janet wearing any of this jewelry other than a small diamond ring."

"What about this one?" asked Elton, pushing a ring across the table.

"Sure looks like it. She wore it all the time. I'm positive about the watch, though."

Rob opened up the album and found some pictures of Grandma Coddington. She was always well dressed and formal in appearance in the photos. They were able to match three pieces of jewelry.

Elton briefed them on the case details. He explained that he thought Jerry must have been in Janet's room, and she caught him stealing her jewelry from her dresser. When she tried to run from the room, Jerry panicked and pulled her back and smothered her. It was not a premeditated act, but it was violent and required time and commitment to accomplish. The element of time necessary to smother a person was disturbing. It was more than a random act of violence. Given the bruising on her left wrist, Jerry must have ripped the watch off her when she was still alive. Rob was quiet as Elton spoke. It was hard to hear the details of his mother's death. She should have died with her friends and family by her side. Not at the hands of a violent criminal.

Jerry finally admitted he had been stealing from the care homes for many years. He would not say when it started, but clearly it was an established pattern. He disposed of most of the stolen items in New

York City. He had developed a relationship with some pawn shops who were not overly interested in where he acquired the items. He also used other shops in the state. He was very careful to spread the items around the state and would never use a shop near the assisted living home where he stole the items. Phil and Elton were lucky in finding Janet's items at his house as he usually did not hold on to any of the stolen goods for long.

It was a surprise that a case can turn on something so simple as looking at actual days rather than dates. You never know when a case will open up, and when it does, all the pieces fall into place.

"I think that if Brian had not shown us this capability of interchanging dates and days we wouldn't have broken the case as quickly as we did," said Elton, "Brian, you get the detective of the year award."

Elton finished up the meeting by explaining to them how the case would unfold in the coming months. "The first stop will be the DA's office and then on to a grand jury. I'm sure we'll get an indictment and go to trial. There may be delaying tactics by the defense, but at some point, the case will go to trial. Now guys, it could be a year or maybe two, but the wheels of justice will prevail. It will be up to the DA as to whether or not there will be a sentence modification if Jerry pleads guilty. Hard to say how she will play it. But take it to the bank, Jerry Monroe is going away for a long, long time, and his wife will face jail time too."

"I'm just happy for the closure Elton. Thank you for making this happen."

Walking out of the police station Brian said to Rob, "Let's go over and see Johnny Forman. The parts are in and Johnny is working on the car."

Johnny's shop was clearly many works in progress. About five cars in various stages of repair. Seems as if John was still taking in multiple jobs pretty much at the same time. In the corner, under a tarp, was the

Edsel. Johnny made a bit of a presentation taking the tarp off the car, sort of like the master of ceremony.

"Ta-dah! I proudly present the best 1960 Edsel Ranger in New York state and maybe the country!"

Rob exclaimed, "John, I had no idea the car would look so good, even at this point. Amazing!"

"Well, Rob, you have a great car to sell here,"

"Where do we go from here?"

Brian responded, "I've been looking at the question and I think we may have a way forward. One of the guys at Edgewood Gardens used to work for a publishing company. They handled a variety of magazines. He told me that most of the articles in them are put together by folks that are called stringers. Basically, they are commissioned by the magazine to write a piece or they develop one themselves and peddle it to the magazines. This guy still has some good contacts and has agreed to contact them and see if they have any interest doing a story on the Edsel. He thinks it will be quite attractive to them as they have a lot of options of where to place it: Car mags, antique mags, and general interest. If Johnny is okay letting the car stay here for a few months when it's finished, we should be able to get the word out. Anyone writing the story will be told to make sure they let their readers know the car is for sale and give Johnny a shout-out too. Good advertising for you, John, not that it looks like you need it!"

"I'm okay with the car living here, and if anyone is interested, they can come by and look it over."

"So," said Brian, "we're going to create a market!"

They had driven over in Brian's car. Brian took Rob back to the police headquarters parking lot to get his truck. When they got there, Rob told him to drop him by a Nissan Sentra.

"Rob, where is your super truck?" He'd noticed Rob usually drove a big pick-up.

"Where else," said Rob, "back in the shop, this is a rental."

Rob continued, "Same problem for the past year or so. Electronics. The dash displays, radio and phone will all be fine and then crash. Totally blank screen. Then after you shut it down and start it up again, you might be back in business. On cold days it is never certain if the good truck or bad truck will appear. I am so tired of this and want to see it sorted out."

Brian asked, "Have you looked into the NY Lemon Law program?"

"No, I've heard the term but don't know anything about it."

"Send me a summary of the situation, and I'll pass it to Brad Petronella at the DA's office. He does Mediations and Lemon Law Arbitrations. I can ask him to take a look at it and see if he thinks you have a case."

"What do I send you?"

"Dates, work orders, purchase date, mileage, stuff like that. New York State Dispute Resolution Association will see if you fit the criteria. If you do, you can file a claim with them and they'll assign an arbitrator to handle the case."

"Is it expensive?" asked Rob.

"Maybe a filing fee but I don't think anything else. The arbitrators are all volunteers."

"Okay, great idea! Thanks! Back to you soon."

Chapter 20

THE TEAM MANAGERS HELD their midseason meeting to see how the program was working. The coaches were happy with the new system as they had a lot more visibility into the mechanics of the teams in terms of equipment, status of the players, and upcoming events. They had a place to go to access the information, and did not have to hunt all over God's creation for data. The team managers loved the system as they were now an integral part of the team. Important to the coaches and also players. After Tommy's speech, you could almost feel the change among the players. They bought into his philosophy of a long-term game plan. The managers were finding that they were important to the players. Not just equipment and schedules, but a source for discussing the plans, hopes, and dreams.

Carly had many long conversations with DeShawn and hooked him up with the new guidance counselor at the school. He and DeShawn met over the course of two months and sorted out an academic schedule that provided, as Tommy said, options!

Carly could see the academic part of DeShawn's life taking over the sports side. One day on the school bus DeShawn said to Carly, "I love sports, but I want a life too!"

Sean could see a rush coming next year with applicants wanting to be part of the team manager program! What a success! Thanks Brian!

The following week, Brian got a large package from Rob. Shop work orders, purchase invoice, mileage history, and a good narrative about the problem. Brian sent it over to Brad Petronella at the Resolution Center. Brad called back shortly to advise that Rob should file a Lemon Law claim with the New York State Dispute Resolution Association in Albany

Rob's pickup truck was a qualified candidate for Lemon Law Arbitration. He met the mileage, repair attempts, and length of ownership. A date was set and an arbitrator assigned. The case would be heard in Albany.

In an arbitration, all the parties are required to submit their supporting documentation known as evidence, ahead of the hearing. Both parties are required to do this. The arbitrator reviews the evidence which forms the basis for the arbitration. Either side can challenge the other party's evidence. Both sides also make an oral presentation of their case and can question each other. Once the oral presentations are finished the arbitrator may decide to look at the vehicle and take a test ride. After that he will close the hearing and has five days to reach a judgement. His judgement is sent to Albany for review and then a verdict is rendered. It's a binding arbitration and short of judicial mistakes, it is the final decision.

Over the years, the Lemon Law has changed in terms of the type of cases arbitrated. In the early days the claims were mainly about engines, transmissions, and suspensions. Now the field had shifted. The problem area these days was mostly electronics. Brad had given this a lot of thought and it seemed that the main problem was that the car companies did not make any of the electronics. It was all purchased equipment and from a number of different manufacturers. By itself it was not a major issue, however, the car companies did not really understand about system integration issues and did not have comprehensive software integration documents tying together all the electronics. Brad felt that the Japanese companies did a better job in this area. Detroit had a way to go.

A field engineer from the car company was part of their arbitration team. After the presentation of evidence from both sides, they started the oral testimonies. Rob had shown that he was repeatedly told by the company that a software fix was in process. It had been over a year and still no fix for the problem.

At this point the field engineer spoke up. "Mr. Coddington, we've let you down. We now have a fix for the problem and should have notified you earlier. I am really sorry for your troubles; we did not support you.

Rob asked, "What was the problem?"

"The backup TV camera."

"Are you kidding me! A TV backup camera shut the whole system down?" exclaimed Rob.

"It sure did. Switching from TV presentation to the other electronics systems on the shared display after backing up locked up the system and effectively shut it down."

Rob asked, "Do you have the new software and parts on hand at the dealerships?"

"Yes, I checked this morning with Henderson's and they have the software and hardware. We want to replace the TV camera also."

Rob was quiet for some time thinking about what he wanted to do. He'd been driving their pickup trucks for twelve years or so and liked their products. On the other hand, they had dropped him in the proverbial bucket of feces by not addressing the problem. So, stay with what you know or start all over again?

Rob said, "I've been with you guys for three pickups, and overall they've been good products. I'm going to give you a get out of jail free card. Today is Tuesday. I want the truck fixed this week, and if you can't do it, I'll take my chances with the arbitrator's decision."

"Mr. Coddington, that's more than fair. Thank you for giving us another chance to put this right. I'll call Henderson's to make sure they will make space for the work and I'll go there also to see it through."

The arbitrator spoke up. "I'll write this up and need to advise you that you also have to return $250 to Mr. Coddington. That was his filing fee."

Rob was happy with the outcome. His truck had very low mileage, and he'd added some custom features and equipment to it that he would not have been able to recover as they were not products of the car company. So maybe it was a win-win.

Chapter 21

BRIAN AND ROB WERE still trying to process Janet's murder. For Brian, a dear friend. For Rob, someone killed his mother. It was more than the fact that they had lost her. It was all so senseless. Stealing jewelry and someone dies? It would take them a long time to come to terms with this mindless violence. But the two men had formed a strong bond and were a source of support for each other. They continued to stay in touch, looking after each other. Brian drew some comfort in knowing that he had helped Elton in solving the case. Rob would be forever grateful to Detective Hendricks for his persistence in solving the case. It could have easily remained an open case and just faded away.

Jerry Monroe agreed with the DA to plead guilty to the charges and was sentenced to twenty-five years in prison. No chance of an early release for good behavior. He would do the time. His wife was sentenced to ten years and would also do the time.

Epilogue

IN MARCEL ARGENTARU'S words, "The team management system is a roaring success!" All the coaches like it and the role of team manager at Binghamton High took on a new meaning. Brian and Carly were asked by other schools around the state to brief them on the system. Brian had a robust software package by this time and they gladly shared it with the other schools. This got Carly thinking about software integration. Maybe this was for her future company.

DeShawn was going into his senior year and his focus had changed from finding a football program to finding a school that supported his long term plans. He talked with Tommy about his plans and the two had developed a close relationship. Tommy and Ruth had three girls, so DeShawn was the big brother the girls loved.

Rob was happy with his truck. Fixed and running well. The big surprise for him was the Edsel. They sold it late in the year for $210,000! Who would have thought? He sent Brian and Johnny a check for $5,000 each and told them that they could not return it. If they did not want to accept the money, then donate it to a charity. Rob also took some of the money from the Edsel and had the garden on the north-side of Edgewood Gardens re-designed with wide, well-lit walks in honor of his mother. She had loved walking there in the evening but had often remarked it was sometimes hard to see when it got dark.

Bill and Maggie were busy presenting their personal property tracking system to other interested care homes. The Edgewood Gardens corporation adopted the system for all their homes. There was also the offer of an article in a nationally distributed magazine.

Brian slowly adjusted to life without Janet. She had been such a part of his life. A big hole to fill. Brad Petronella had called him. He was doing some casework for the DA and wanted Brian to help him sort and present some data. His CPA background was a big asset. Mary Louise was happy to have him and agreed to bring him onboard and on-call as other cases came through. He called Tommy to let him know of this new development.

"Pop, you are a secret agent now. Go get them bad guys!"

Sean McCarthy's team beat Elmira in the opening game and went on to the state playoffs.

The End

If you've enjoyed this book, please leave a review. It is really helpful for a beginning author. The link is below.

Please go to my website for more information about my Upstate
Mysteries and a FREE short story
https://upstatemysteries.godaddysites.com/

Don't miss out!

Visit the website below and you can sign up to receive emails whenever fj donohue publishes a new book. There's no charge and no obligation.

https://books2read.com/r/B-A-CFSO-OKGPB

BOOKS2READ

Connecting independent readers to independent writers.

Also by fj donohue

Endwell Investigations
Full Circle
Vindication

Upstate Mystery
Hit and Run
Two Murders by the River
A Serial Killer Returns
Right Time Wrong Place
The Caribbean Laundry

Upstate Mystery #2
Closure

Upstate Mystery #7
The Snowbird Bank Robber

Watch for more at https://upstatemystery.com.

About the Author

I'm a retired International Sales Director, having worked in the commercial and military flight simulation industry for over 30 years. I lived in Brussels (Belgium) and Bonn (Germany) for eight years and met my British wife in Brussels. Before my career in the flight simulation industry, I was an Armaments and Electronics Maintenance Officer in the USAF during the Viet Nam era conflict. We have three children and seven grandchildren.

Since retirement I continue to chase an ever-elusive golf game.

Home is a small town in central New York State where the novellas are set.

I'm a volunteer mediator and Lemon Law arbitrator and this occasionally appears in the stories. An underlying theme in my novellas is people helping people. In spite of the difficulties and crime that may surround us, there is always hope in friendship and good neighbors.

Go to my website below for information about my novellas and to contact me for a FREE short story. I won't use your information for any other purpose.

Read more at https://upstatemystery.com.

www.ingramcontent.com/pod-product-compliance
Lightning Source LLC
Chambersburg PA
CBHW022205150726
47992CB00002B/967